The Screaming Demon Ghostie

People said, "You're new here, Kate. Keep off that old forest track after night falls." Their eyes swivelled like ball bearings while they looked around, then they tickled her ear as they hissed, "The Screaming Demon Ghostie of the old forest track could grab you!"

Dare you try *another* Young Hippo Spooky?

Scarem's House
Malcolm Yorke

Three Young Hippo Magic stories to enjoy:

The Little Pet Dragon
Philippa Gregory

The Marmalade Pony
Linda Newbery

My Friend's a Gris-Quok
Malorie Blackman

Ready for a Young Hippo Adventure?

Henry to the Rescue and Other Stories
Ruth Silvestre

Young Hippo Adventures for confident readers:

The Outfit Series –
The Secret of Weeping Wood
We Didn't Mean To, Honest!
Robert Swindells

JEAN CHAPMAN

The Screaming Demon
Ghostie

Inside illustrations by David Cox

Scholastic Children's Books,
Scholastic Publications Ltd,
7–9 Pratt Street, London NW1 0AE, UK

Scholastic Inc.,
555 Broadway, New York, NY 10012-3999, USA

Scholastic Canada Ltd,
123 Newkirk Road, Richmond Hill,
Ontario, Canada L4C 3G5

Ashton Scholastic Pty Ltd,
P O Box 579, Gosford, New South Wales,
Australia

Ashton Scholastic Ltd,
Private Bag 92801, Penrose, Auckland,
New Zealand

First published in Australia by Omnibus Books, part of the
ASHTON SCHOLASTIC GROUP, 1992

First published in the UK by Scholastic Children's Books, 1994

Text copyright © Jean Chapman, 1992
Inside illustrations copyright © David Cox, 1992
Cover illustration copyright © Philip Hopman, 1994

ISBN 0 590 55812 9

Typeset by Contour Typesetters, Southall, London
Printed by Cox & Wyman Ltd, Reading, Berks.

10 9 8 7 6 5 4 3 2 1

For P. and J. and J.

Some time ago, Kate Kelly landed a fine job with none other than Sir Merino. He was just home from abroad. All alone, young and lonely in his big echoing house, he needed someone to cook for him. "You can live in the little hut off the old forest track down the hill," he told Kate.

Kate was over the moon with delight until people said, "You're new here, Kate. Keep off that old forest track after night falls." Their eyes swivelled like ball bearings while they looked around, then they tickled her ear as they hissed, "The Screaming Demon Ghostie of the old forest track could grab you!"

"OOOOH!" moaned Kate. In her mind's eye she saw its alarming bigness, its dreadful whiteness and its bony see-throughness. In her mind's ear she could hear the wild shrieks of the Screaming Demon Ghostie.

She told Sir Merino about it.

"In all my born days, I've never heard such rot," he said. "Absolute nonsense, Kate."

"But sir, the Screaming Demon Ghostie is big like your house," whispered Kate. "It would frighten you silly to see it."

Smiley eyes met Kate's. "If that's so, let's hope we don't meet it. Still, it wouldn't frighten me. Nothing frightens me, Kate – nothing! Now, just leave me a bite to eat each evening, then home you go before dark."

He's such a lovely man, she thought, and on summer evenings she left his meal under a cage hooded with netting. In winter it steamed on the wood stove.

Always Kate skipped off home down the old forest track before dark. She never saw the Screaming Demon Ghostie. Never heard a squeak. Perhaps the story was rot. Kate longed to be sure.

Everything was hunky-dory until Sir Merino had a birthday. He planned a party with lots of food. And a four-layered chocolate, cream and raspberry jam cake. With tiny silvery balls on the pink icing. Kate willingly made everything on the day before the birthday. She was still working at nightfall, and she started off home in black darkness.

It was as black as the bottom of a coal mine when she took her first steps on the old forest track. Spooky-quiet, too. Then, close to home, Kate stumbled. Her feet went everywhere. WHAM! She landed on her behind, half on top of something hard like a rock.

She felt its shape. It was an old camp oven, for sure. Left behind by some traveller, and full of rusty holes.

Then, lo and behold, the moon dipped out from behind a cloud. Kate saw that it was indeed an old oven. Thinking that she could grow a plant in it, she said, "I'll take you home."

"NO, YOU WON'T!" The shriek came
straight from the oven. Kate's ears, her
head and the air about her were filled with
it. The moon tried to hide.

A face-paling thing, groaning and moaning, flung itself at Kate. She froze. She couldn't even cry out. Her insides leaped about under her pinny.

The Screaming Demon Ghostie sprang closer, too close. Kate staggered to her feet, her heart thumping.

Again it rushed at Kate with woe-filled cries. She couldn't understand one word.

Kate started to run. The Screaming Demon Ghostie blocked her way, no matter where she turned. She dodged and ducked. She tripped over ruts, into potholes. Still, she kept away from it. Just. It was everywhere.

Kate stood still, panting. The moon shone again, bright and full. At least now she could see better.

"YAHHHHH!" The Screaming Demon Ghostie pulled an awful face.

Kate laughed, her fear slipping away. "That's a silly face. Don't you know that if the wind changes you'll stay like that?" She was herself again. "However did you get into that oven?"

The Screaming Demon Ghostie hung its head. It wavered about and seemed to shrink. Heavens! worried Kate. It might fade away! The Screaming Demon Ghostie was not as she'd imagined. Suddenly she was sorry for it, and she said quickly, "I don't want your oven. You keep it."

"It's not my oven. I had to hide some-where when you came," it whispered. Then it waily-wailed like a cat: "I'm a terrible f-f-f-failure! I don't properly scare anyone. And when I tried to run off, you were in my w-w-way."

Kate was astonished. Fancy anything being afraid of her!

"You scared *me*," she told it, but the ghostie was whispering again, as humble as one of Kate's old spuds: "Until tonight I've always hidden away in the thick forest where no one ever goes. I've never had a proper place to haunt. I've been so l-l-lonely." And it waily-wailed again.

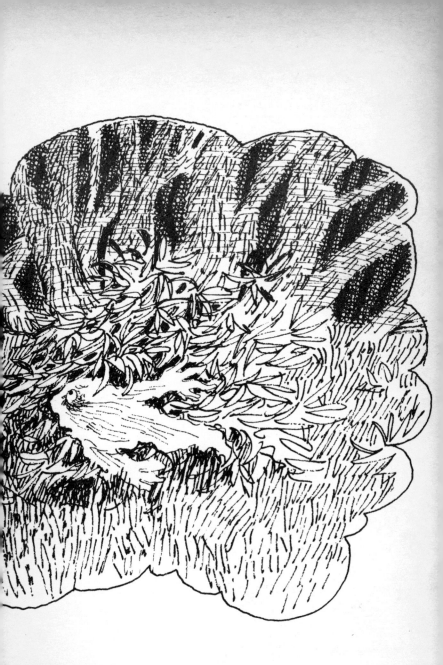

"Oh, you poor thing! You need a friend," Kate said. "Come home with me. We'll have some milky tea with honey bread," she promised, scooping up the ghostie in her arms. Well, it was hardly taller than a teddy bear, and no heavier than half a cup of flour.

She carried the ghostie to her cottage, settled it in her own soft chair on the softest cushion, lit the fire, and soon offered it milky tea and honey bread.

Just as Kate enjoyed her first sips of hot tea, a sudden thud-thud-thud shook the door. She jumped: her cup rattled on its saucer. "Who's there?" she squeaked.

The ghostie, even more startled than Kate, flipped off the chair and slid down behind it – hiding again.

"Are you all right, Kate?" roared Sir Merino, outside and unafraid in the night.

How Kate beamed as she answered the door. "I'm all right," she chirped. "Do come in."

He burst in like a shot, filling the room with his hearty voice. "I went to the kitchen, Kate, so that I could escort you home down the old forest track. But you'd gone off into the dark by yourself." He looked sheepish. "I just wanted to be sure you were home safely. I know how you feel about the Screaming Demon Ghostie," he added, with a teasing smile.

"Oh, but I did meet a ghostie," Kate told him.

"The Screaming Demon Ghostie? Come now, Katie girl." Sir Merino laughed down at her. "I can't believe that. There's no such thing."

"I don't tell fibs," flared Kate. "I did meet a ghostie – but never a Screaming Demon Ghostie." Her indignant eyes met his. "Do you agree that seeing is believing?"

Sir Merino still grinned. Confidence almost sparked off him. "Of course," he nodded, settling himself in Kate's own chair.

"Sir Merino, here is my friend, the ghostie from the thick forest where no one ever goes." She drew the ghostie from its hiding place.

Puzzled, Sir Merino looked about the room. He didn't see the ghostie shyly drifting about Kate's knees. That wasn't surprising. A wispy enough thing in the lamplight, the ghostie had faded until it was even more see-through, nervous to meet another huge alive-alive-o person so soon.

"Oh, Kate!" Sir Merino was sure that Kate was teasing him.

"Ghostie, dear," crooned Kate, "could you show yourself to Sir Merino?"

A little flurry caught Sir Merino's eye as something flicked into his vision and hovered an arm's length away.

"Good evening," whispered a voice. It was not Kate's.

Sir Merino's face turned the colour of an uncooked apple pie. He did not want to believe his eyes. He drew back against the chair. His hands gripped its arms as he gawped at the ghostie.

A gluggy gurgle, just like water going down a plug-hole, rumbled from Sir Merino. He sagged limp as a wet dish-cloth as Kate jigged before him, holding a . . . a . . . perfect little ghost!

"You're not a failure, ghostie," she sang. "You've frightened Sir Merino now! Just look at him!"

When she looked
herself, she was dis-
mayed to see the state
he was in. She rushed to
his side. She fanned his face,
patted his cheeks, rubbed his hands,
and just as he was becoming himself
again, she kissed him on top of his head.

In that very moment Sir Merino knew that he believed in ghosts, at least in Kate's. He gazed at her, his heart soaring. She was the most lovely-lovely girl in the world. He'd marry her one day.

Sir Merino's face soon returned to its own natural colour. He looked hard at the ghostie. "This must be our secret," he declared.

"Why?" wondered the ghostie.

"You'd soon be headlines in all the papers, and everyone would be rushing here to meet you," Sir Merino warned it. "You could end up in a sideshow, or in a scientist's specimen jar. You'd hate that."

"Never that!" cried Kate, aghast. "Stay here! Be our secret friend for ever."

"Kate and I will look after you," Sir Merino decided, as if they'd settled everything.

"Oh yes," purred the ghostie, glowing with joy. And it never waily-wailed again, now that it knew it wasn't a spooky failure.

The next evening the ghostie had a
lovely time at the birthday party, flitting
here and there. It even dared to offer
cake, then sailed off to enjoy the astonished looks on guests' faces. Ah yes, the
ghostie was almost invisible in the bright
light of Sir Merino's chandelier with its
forty lit candles.

In fact, it hardly saw itself when it accidentally bumped into the huge mirror over the fireplace. It couldn't resist pulling a face in the glass, then. A ghastly ghostly face, as hideous as the one it had made at Kate.

Then, all at once, the ghostie had a beautiful thought. "Oh, bliss!" it chuckled. "At last! At last! I've a lovely, a truly proper place to haunt!"

The ghostie went
on happily flitting
about Sir Merino's
big house long after
Sir Merino and
Kate were married,
and it became the
secret friend of their
children and their
children's children.

And, of course, you've guessed! Folk went on telling stories about the Screaming Demon Ghostie of the old forest track. No one ever walked there alone after dark. Yet the ghost was nothing more than the moonlight gliding in and out of trees. Such things can make some folk nervous. They see what isn't there. And it's squirrels squabbling and screeching that turn their knees to jelly, for sure.

The End

**Dare you read *another*
Young Hippo Spooky?**

Scarem's House
Malcolm Yorke

The Merry family went out slamming the old door shut behind them, and the ghostly O'Gools were left in a state of shock.

Scarem was also furious. "My ancestors built this house and now these humans are just going to sell it over our heads! It's already occupied! By us! Don't ghosts have any rights at all?"

When Scarem O'Gool's house is invaded by humans, there's only one solution. They'll have to be *haunted* out!

YOUNG HiPPO MAGIC

Magic is in the air with these enchanting stories
from Young Hippo Magic – stories about ordinary,
everyday children who discover that in the world of
magic, anything is possible!

The Little Pet Dragon
Philippa Gregory

James is thrilled when he finds a tiny greyhound
puppy! But aren't those scales on its body? And
isn't that snouty face rather dragon-like? James
doesn't notice, because his puppy is glimmering
with a very strong magic . . .

My Friend's a Gris-Quok
Malorie Blackman

A Young Hippo Magic story for early readers

Alex has a deep, dark secret. He's half Gris-Quok,
which is fantastic, because he can turn himself into
anything he likes! However, he can only do it *three*
times a day . . .

The Marmalade Pony
Linda Newbery

A Young Hippo Magic story for early readers

Hannah has always longed for a pony of her very
own, but the best she can do is imagine. Then one
day her dad starts making something mysterious in
the shed . . .

The Outfit

Robert Swindells

"Faithful, fearless, full of fun,
Winter, summer, rain or sun,
One for five, and five for one –
THE OUTFIT!"

Meet The Outfit—Jillo, Titch, Mickey and Shaz. Share in their adventures as they fearlessly investigate any mystery, and injustice, that comes their way . . .

Move over, Famous Five, The Outfit are here!

The Secret of Weeping Wood

The Outfit are determined to discover the truth about the eerie crying, coming from scary Weeping Wood. Is the wood really haunted?

We Didn't Mean To, Honest!

The marriage of creepy Kenneth Kilchaffinch to snooty Prunella could mean that Froglet Pond, and all its wildlife, will be destroyed. So it's up to The Outfit to make sure the marriage is off . . . But how?

Kidnap at Denton Farm

Farmer Denton's new wind turbine causes a protest meeting in Lenton, and The Outfit find themselves in the thick of it. But a *kidnap* is something they didn't bargain for . . .

The Ghosts of Givenham Keep

What is going on at spooky Givenham Keep? It can't be haunted, can it? The Outfit are just about to find out . . .